INDEX

The Clever Wife	3
Raghu	5, 57, 98
Did You Know?	6, 68, 125
Say It Yourself	7, 69, 126
Editor's Choice	8, 34, 96, 127, 154
Nasruddin Hodja	9, 36
Above and Below	10
The Ungrateful Master	12
Our Windows to the World	16
Two Crabs	18
Shikari Shambu	19, 81, 138
The Bag of Jewellery	22
Meet the Chicken	28
The Most Precious Pearl	31
Say Hello to Maranna V. Shetty	
Results of the Story Competition	33
Mooshik	5, 35, 67, 97, 124, 155
Tinkle Tricks & Treats	37, 99, 157
Make a Colourful Dustbin	38
The Monkey's Dance	39
The Sun	43
How the Titeeri Took to Water	46
Miserly Wit	49
Kalia the Crow	50, 112
The Employer Who Didn't Want to Pay	53
Odd Friends- I	58
The Trick That Failed	60
The Wise King	62
Vinu	64
Anwar	66, 123
About Say It Yourself	

INDEX

Pakodas for the Bear	71
Humidity	75
Eggs	76
Two Sisters	78
A Helping Hand	80
Chetak	84
Wit of Vijayaraj	90
Odd Friends- II	91
The Singing Peacock	93
Say Hello to Sulabha Thakur	
The Clever Rabbit	101
Complete the Story: The Knock	102
The Sun-ll	103
The Barber Meets a Tiger	106
The Deserving One	109
Silk Cotton Tree	111
How Plants Are Born	115
Ramu and the Rickshaw	118
The Show-off	119
Lazy Raghu	121
The Resourceful Rani	128
An Army of Dogs	132
About Raghu	
The Stethoscope	135
A Wolf Sings!	137
Shoes for a Tower	141
The Fisherman and His Daughters	142
Meet the Earthworm	148
The Magic Mirror	151
Readers Write	156

As a child enthralled by *Tinkle*, there was hardly anything in the magazine I didn't adore. I say 'hardly' because there was this one thing that I then disliked intensely but now find fascinating—the knowledge features! Now I can't figure out the reason for my then aversion, for the column is full of the most interesting facts and illustrations. And yet, I remember one knowledge feature about onions that held my attention. I was stunned to read that onions were once given as valuable wedding gifts in medieval times! It made me look at onions quite differently from then on!

A feature that I absolutely looked forward to was 'This Happened to Me'. It was like reading a series of jokes (all mostly based on mishaps!) crossed with a sort of pen pal column. Children from across the country wrote in to *Tinkle* about various funny incidents in their lives. For a child in Mumbai, it felt like receiving funny letters from places as diverse as Jammu, Dibrugarh, Calicut, Vadodara, Ludhiana or Imphal. So it is not very surprising that this feature remains a favourite. Now called 'It Happened to Me', in a recent content survey we ran among young readers, this column emerged as the second most popular one.

Then there were the letters from Uncle Pai. It felt like he was talking to me alone. As if I was as important as an adult. This was a big deal in my world as a child where most of my questions were dismissed with—"You'll understand when you're older". Sometimes Uncle Pai narrated a story with a moral, at other times he related a funny story sent by another reader. And always, he signed off with an 'affectionately yours'. As a child I thought one had to be extra special to get one of these letters from the great Uncle Pai.

Today, when I'm in this surreal space of being in the editor's chair, I know how it feels to be at the other end. Perhaps the child of today may not have the sense of wonder that infused the child of the 1980s or even the 1990s. But what remains is the bluntness that comes through in an email from a child. The child has no other motive than to simply scold the editor for a story that didn't make them happy or to share the joy of a story well loved. This is why feedback from readers is so sought after and looked forward to.

Tinkle has seen the change from the old millennium to the new—stories, writers, artists and readers. As you turn these pages may fond memories come to you and may you help spread the magic.

Happy reading,
Rajani Thindiath
Editor-in-Chief, *Tinkle*

"The content including the information, pictures, offers, contests and prizes is reproduced from the October 1983 to January 1984 editions of *Tinkle* No. 45 to 50 in its original and unaltered form to retain the essence of *Tinkle* Origins. Some of the facts may have been changed as of this day. Neither the offers nor prizes are currently valid. Any participation or claim in this regard shall not be entertained."

```
EDITOR-IN-CHIEF      :  RAJANI THINDIATH
GROUP ART DIRECTOR   :  SAVIO MASCARENHAS
EDITORIAL TEAM       :  SEAN D'MELLO, APARNA SUNDARESAN,
                        RITU MAHIMKAR, AASHLINE ROSE AVARACHAN,
                        JUBEL D'CRUZ, POOJA WAGHELA
HEAD OF CREATIVE SERVICES : KURIAKOSE SAJU VAISIAN
DESIGN TEAM          :  TARUN SOMANATHAN, KETAN TONDWALKAR
COVER DESIGN         :  AKSHAY KHADILKAR
```

© Amar Chitra Katha Pvt. Ltd., May 2019, ISBN 978-93-88957-07-6
AFL House, 7th Floor, Lok Bharti Complex, Marol, Andheri (East), Mumbai – 400059
Tel: +91 22 4918 888 1/2 | Fax: +91 22 4918 8802
www.tinkle.in | www.amarchitrakatha.com

Printed at M/s Spenta Multimedia Pvt. Ltd., Peninsula Spenta, 2nd Floor,
Mathuradas Mill Compound, Lower Parel (West), Mumbai – 400013.

Get in touch with us:

© Amar Chitra Katha Pvt. Ltd.
This book is sold subject to the condition that the publication may not be reproduced, stored in a retrieval system (including but not limited to computers, disks, external drives, electronic or digital devices, e-readers, websites), or transmitted in any form or by any means (including but not limited to cyclostyling, photocopying, docutech or other reprographic reproductions, mechanical, recording, electronic, digital versions) without the prior written permission of the publisher, nor be otherwise circulated in any form of binding or cover other than that in which it is published and without a similar condition being imposed on the subsequent purchaser.

THE CLEVER WIFE

Readers' Choice — Illustrations: Bapu Patil

Based on a story sent by Sanjay Kumar Jain, Kachiguda

Raghu
Based on an idea suggested by V. Venkatesh, Bangalore

Readers Write...

I am in Std. VI now. A week after school started our teacher asked if anyone of us read TINKLE. I said I did and the next day I brought a copy of TINKLE to class. While the teacher read it carefully, we got a free period! She liked it very much!

Bipin Kaoray
Bombay

TINKLE comes very late to my town – sometimes it takes 10 days and sometimes 15. It is also the magazine which gets sold out first in every bookstall in Ranchi. So please see that TINKLE is sent earlier and that you send many more copies.

Sharad Poddar
Ranchi

TINKLE is really an interesting magazine. I came back from abroad last month and was longing to read a good magazine in India. I am very glad to say that I have found a magazine in India which is better than any American magazine I have ever come across. I am sending TINKLE to my friends in the States now. Let's see what they say.

Himanoj Tyagi
Agra

My brother and I get confused with the TINKLE number and dates. I say we have bought the latest issue (No. 38) and he says that we haven't bought the July issue; so could you please publish the date on the front cover?

Radhika Kelkar
Bombay

Mooshik
Based on an idea suggested by Venkateshwara Rao and Praveen Kumar, Hyderabad

DID YOU KNOW?

Cotton was first grown in India 5000 years ago. Indian cotton textiles were being exported to other lands at the time of the Indus Valley Civilization (3000-2000 BC).

Egyptian mummies are said to have been wrapped in Indian muslin and ladies of ancient Rome fancied Indian textiles.

When Alexander and his Greek armies invaded the Punjab in 327 BC and saw cotton bolls for the first time, they thought it was wool growing on trees.

COTTON

Common English words which refer to cotton textiles — calico, chintz, dungaree, pyjama, sash and gingham — are all of Indian origin.

EDITOR'S CHOICE

My young friends,

A fir tree and a bramble bush lived near each other on the top of a hill. The proud fir tree used to taunt the bramble bush: "Look at me! I am tall and graceful and very beautiful. You, you puny thing, are so small and untidy, and very ugly!"

The poor, unhappy bramble bush could find no answer to these rude remarks made by the fir tree. Because it thought that the fir tree was right – the bush did feel small and untidy!

But one day some men came up the hill, carrying axes. They began to chop down the tall fir tree as they needed wood to build houses.

"Oh dear!" cried the fir tree as it began to fall. "I wish I were a bramble bush, then men would not cut me down!"

The proud fir tree fell with a thud, but the bramble bush continued to stand where it always had!

Master Firdaus Byramji from Secunderabad sent me this story to share with all of you.

Affectionately yours,

Anant Pai

Uncle Pai

Nasruddin Hodja

RESULTS OF SAY IT YOURSELF* No.2

* Refer to the footnote under the Editor's Note

FIRST PRIZE: (Rs.50)
Jacob Paul, 19, Sargent House, Barrow Road, Bombay 400 039.

SECOND PRIZE: (Rs.25)
Hema Thakore, 10, Namrata Housing Society, Stadium Road, Ahmedabad 380 014.

THIRD PRIZE: (Rs.15)
Clive Pereira, 303, Sarup Sagar, Prof. Almeida Road, Bandra, Bombay 400 050.

Consolation Prizes: (Rs. 10 each)

Nomita Mehta Bombay	**Bijal A. Damania** Bombay
Roma D. Virginkar Goa	**Reginald Goveas** Bangalore
Anup Agarwalla Bombay	**Maya Venugopalan** Madras
Arun Coelho Prabhu Bombay	**Debasish Das** Kharagpur
Santhosh Thazhathu Bangalore	**Amit Banerjee** Calcutta

Prize-winning entry from Jacob Paul, Bombay.

ABOVE AND BELOW

Story by: J. S. Iyer
Illustrations: Dilip Kadam

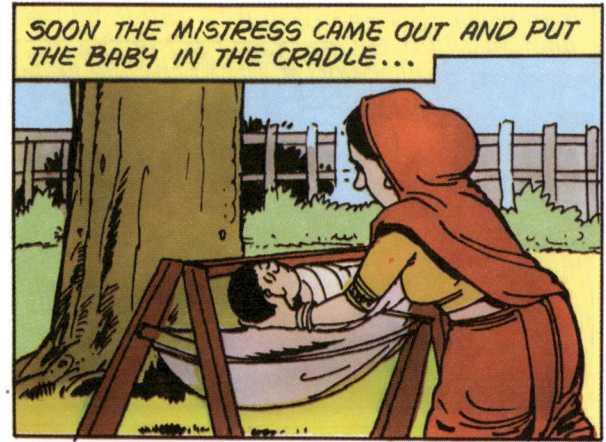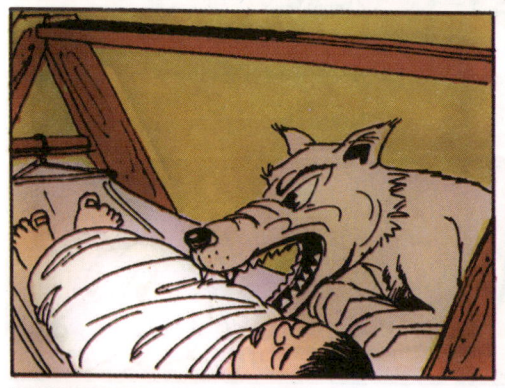

OUR WINDOWS TO THE WORLD
Illustrations: Anand Mande

Though we look with our eyes, it is with our brain that we see. A nerve from the brain called the optic nerve comes to the eyeball and spreads itself out on the rear two-thirds of the eyeball to form the retina. The optic nerve is accompanied by an artery and vein. The artery and the vein spread over the retina.

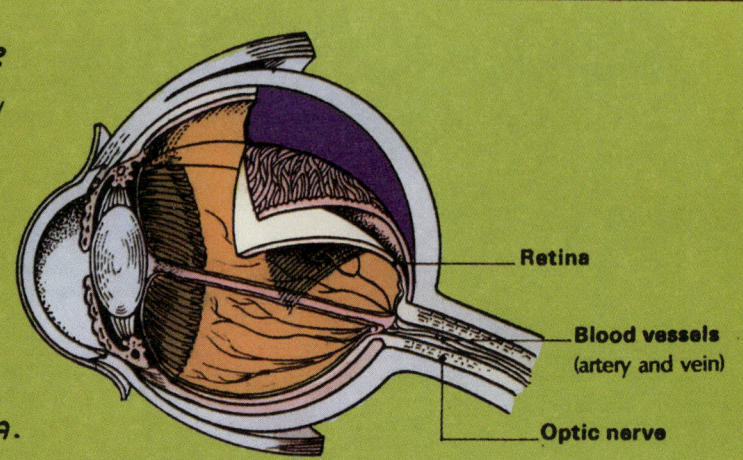

A portion of the front of the eyeball is transparent and this is called the cornea.

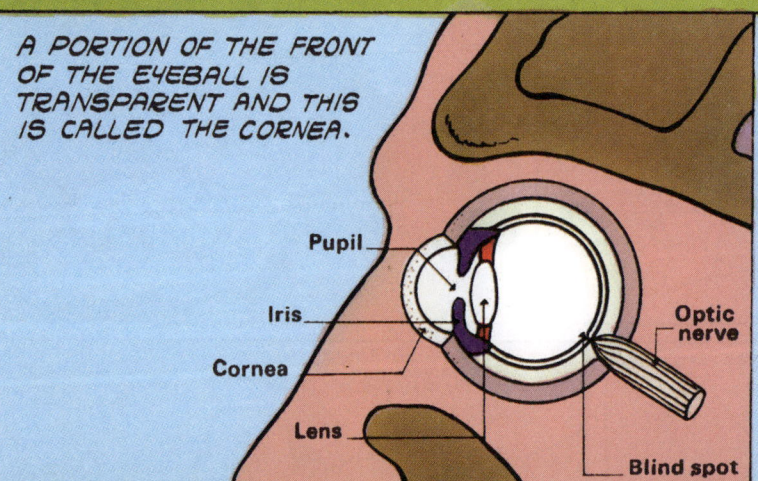

Inside the eyeball are the iris, the pupil and the lens. Between the cornea and the lens there is a watery liquid and between the lens and the back of the eyeball there is a sticky, jelly-like fluid.

There are six muscles which control the movements of each eye.

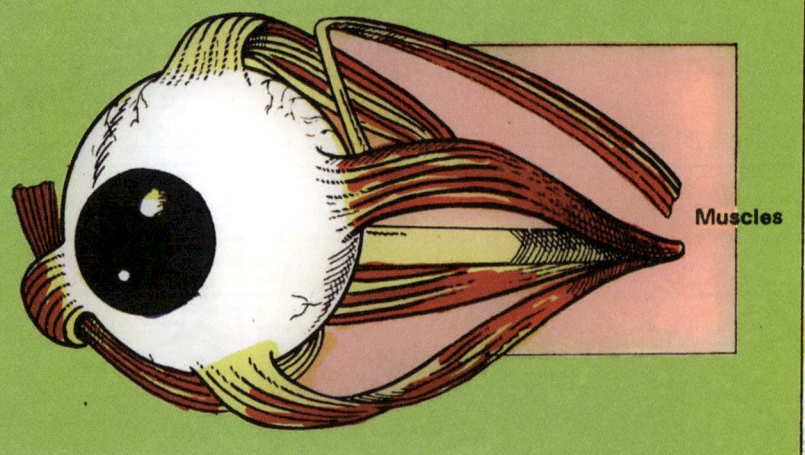

LIGHT FROM THE OBJECT ENTERS THE EYE THROUGH THE PUPIL. THE LIGHT THEN PASSES THROUGH THE LENS AND FALLS ON THE RETINA. AN UPSIDE DOWN PICTURE OF THE OBJECT IS FORMED HERE. A MESSAGE ABOUT THE PICTURE IS THEN SENT TO THE BRAIN THROUGH THE OPTIC NERVE AND THE BRAIN TELLS US WHAT WE ARE LOOKING AT.

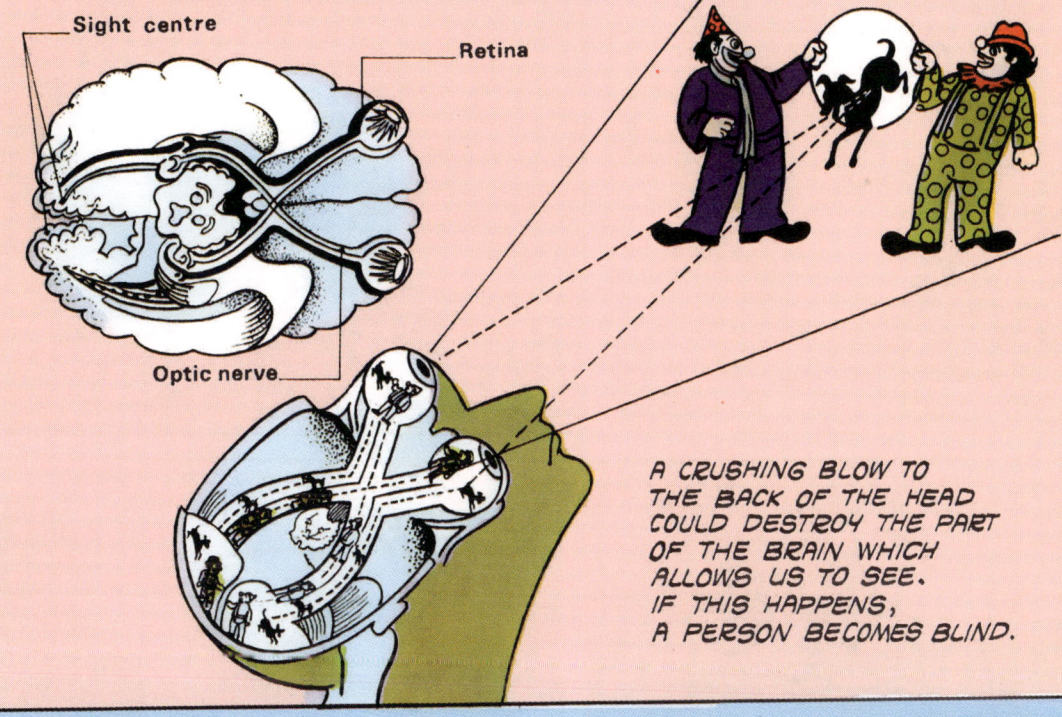

A CRUSHING BLOW TO THE BACK OF THE HEAD COULD DESTROY THE PART OF THE BRAIN WHICH ALLOWS US TO SEE. IF THIS HAPPENS, A PERSON BECOMES BLIND.

A PICTURE IS FORMED ON THE RETINA BECAUSE IT CONTAINS MILLIONS OF CELLS OF A SPECIAL TYPE (RODS AND CONES). THESE CELLS ARE MISSING AT THE POINT WHERE THE OPTIC NERVE ENTERS THE EYE. SO AT THAT PARTICULAR SPOT, THE EYE IS BLIND.

MAKE A DOT AND A CROSS ABOUT 8 CM. APART ON A PIECE OF PAPER. HOLD THE PAPER AT ARM'S LENGTH. SHUT YOUR LEFT EYE AND LOOK AT THE DOT WITH YOUR RIGHT EYE. AS YOU DO SO, BRING THE PAPER TOWARDS YOUR EYES, VERY SLOWLY. ALTHOUGH YOU ARE LOOKING AT THE DOT YOU CAN STILL SEE THE CROSS. THEN AT A CERTAIN POINT THE CROSS SUDDENLY VANISHES. BRING THE PAPER FORWARD AND THE CROSS REAPPEARS. WHY DOES THE CROSS SEEM TO DISAPPEAR? IT DISAPPEARS BECAUSE AT THAT PARTICULAR DISTANCE AND ANGLE, LIGHT FROM THE CROSS IS FALLING DIRECTLY ON THE BLIND SPOT.

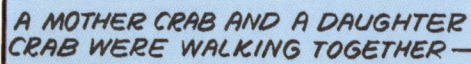

MEET THE CHICKEN

Script and Illustrations: Pradeep Sathe

WHEN YOU GO TO A SHOP TO BUY EGGS, YOU FIND TWO HEAPS OF THEM. ONE HEAP IS CALLED 'DESI' THE OTHER ONE 'ENGLISH'.

'DESI' MEANS NATIVE OR LOCAL. 'DESI' EGGS ARE EGGS LAID BY DESI (LOCAL) HENS.

THE SO-CALLED ENGLISH EGGS ARE EGGS LAID BY A SPECIAL BREED OF CHICKENS CALLED 'WHITE LEGHORNS'. THIS BREED IS VERY POPULAR IN POULTRIES OF OUR COUNTRY.

THE WHITE LEGHORN IS ORIGINALLY FROM ITALY.

NOW LET'S TAKE A LOOK AT OTHER BREEDS OF CHICKENS WHICH ARE EQUALLY POPULAR IN POULTRIES.

Buff Leghorn

Rhode Island Red

Plymouth Rock

Black Minorka

Sussex

Cochin

*Refer to the footnote under the Editor's Note

THOUGH THE BIRD HAS BEEN TAMED FOR CENTURIES, IT HAS NOT FORGOTTEN SOME OF THE HABITS OF ITS ANCESTORS. THE ROOSTER STILL CROWS. THOUGH IN A POULTRY FARM HE HAS NO TERRITORY OF HIS OWN.

BUT THEY HAVE CHANGED IN SOME WAYS.
WHITE LEGHORN HENS, FOR EXAMPLE, HAVE FORGOTTEN HOW TO HATCH EGGS. AND THEY JUST KEEP LAYING EGGS THROUGHOUT THE YEAR. (ABOUT 340 EGGS A YEAR). THAT IS WHY THIS BREED IS POPULAR.

IF THE POULTRY OWNERS WANT TO HATCH THE EGGS THEY DO SO IN ELECTRICAL INCUBATORS.

IF A DOZEN HENS, NEW TO EACH OTHER, ARE PUT TOGETHER THEY WILL START FIGHTING. AFTER SOME TIME THEY COME TO KNOW WHO IS THE STRONGEST HEN, AND THE NEXT STRONGEST AND SO ON.

EVER AFTERWARDS, HEN NO. 1 (THE STRONGEST HEN) CAN PECK ALL THE OTHER HENS, BUT THE OTHER HENS CAN'T PECK HER. HEN NO. 2 CAN PECK ALL OTHER HENS EXCEPT NO. 1. HEN NO. 3 CAN PECK ALL HENS EXCEPT HENS NOS. 1 AND 2. IN THIS WAY A PECKING ORDER IS ESTABLISHED. HEN NO. 12 IS THE WEAKEST HEN. EVERYONE CAN PECK HER, AND SHE CAN'T PECK BACK.

THE ROOSTER ON THE OTHER HAND, CAN PECK ANY HEN IN THE YARD.

* Refer to the footnote under the Editor's Note

THESE TWO ARE NOT POULTRY BIRDS!

THE ASSIL
THIS BREED IS SPECIALLY RAISED FOR FIGHTING. COCK FIGHTING IS A COMMON SPORT IN MANY PARTS OF INDIA.

THE YAKOHAMA
(FROM THE FAR EAST)
THIS IS A SHOW-BIRD. THE ROOSTER HAS VERY LONG TAIL-FEATHERS, MORE THAN 3 METRES.

The Most Precious Pearl

Readers' Choice

Illustrations: Ashok Dongre

Based on a story sent by Upendra Singh, Manipur

IN THE COURT OF THE CALIPH OF BAGHDAD—

DO YOU KNOW WHOM AMONG US THE CALIPH LOVES THE MOST?

YES!

THAT DWARF

WHY ARE YOU SO FOND OF THAT DWARF, O CALIPH?

HE IS SO UGLY!

HE IS FAITHFUL! LISTEN TO WHAT HAPPENED ONCE, MANY YEARS AGO.

★ Refer to the footnote under the Editor's Note

"OUR CARAVAN WAS TRAVELLING THROUGH THE STREETS OF BASRA..."

"...WHEN SUDDENLY A CAMEL SLIPPED AND CAME DOWN IN A HEAP. PRECIOUS PEARLS FROM A CASKET IT WAS CARRYING WERE STREWN ALL OVER..."

SAY HELLO TO BHAVANI SHANKAR GORAY

While speaking to Mr. Subba Rao about the role of Bhavani Shankar Goray with regards to *Tinkle* and *Amar Chitra Katha*, he constantly referred to Mr. Goray as an artist. This initially confounded the team at *Tinkle* as Mr. Goray was always believed to be a letterist and colourist. It was only when Mr. Rao clarified that Mr. Goray was in fact an artist, just not an illustrator that things started to clear up.

You see, Mr. Goray joined *Tinkle* at a time when the processes of colouring and lettering were quite tedious. There were no computers present, every story was lettered by hand. Each letter of the alphabet needed to be painstakingly drawn, ensuring there was enough space for the next. No easy task and one that couldn't afford any errors.

Colouring the pages of *Tinkle* was another tedious task. At the start, a tracing paper was put over the initial inked pages. The colourist would fill in the white spaces and avoid the lines. This process would take a while, something that was not lost on Mr. Goray. He was the first to suggest the use of a camera to photograph these pages. The photographed pages could then be coloured freely without worrying about destroying the originals. This process was revolutionary and dramatically improved the colours of the stories.

It's no wonder then that Mr. Goray is referred to as an artist by his peers. He may not have illustrated stories but he certainly helped bring them to life.

Results of the Complete-the-Story Competition held in the issue of August 5, 1983 *

We got a record number of entries for this competition. But almost all the entries mentioned that the tree was knocked down by the elephant, making a bridge which allowed the man to get down on the other side and escape. But a few were different. To three of the most original, we have given prizes.

First Prize:
J. Meera
c/o P.N. Jagannathan
No.5, Ayavoo Street
Shenoy Nagar
Madras 600 030

THE CHASE
The prize-winning entry:

The man, whose name was Hira Lal, did not know that the elephant was running away from a tiger. The elephant dashed blindly against the tree and fell down, stunned. At the same time, Hira Lal who was on top of the tree, was knocked down. Falling, he landed on the back of the tiger which was chasing the elephant. The surprised tiger, not knowing what was on top of it, jumped across the gap. In fear, it kept running with Hira Lal clinging on to it. It passed through a village and all the villagers stared in wonder at this strange sight of a man riding on the back of a tiger.

Outside the village, the tiger got rid of its burden and ran away. The dazed Hira Lal walked back to the village, where everyone greeted him as a hero. Hira Lal's name was changed to Hero Lal!!

Consolation Prizes:
A consolation prize of Rs. 25/- each has been awarded to
Aniruddha A. Joshi
of Bombay and
Audhoot N. Pai Lotliker
of Bombay

* Refer to the footnote under the Editor's Note

Mooshik
Based on an idea suggested by S. Parthasarathy, Coimbatore

To Our Readers*

TINKLE SUBSCRIPTIONS:
All new subscriptions and renewals of the old ones are accepted at:
PARTHA BOOKS DIVISION
Nav Prabhat Chambers, Ranade Road, Dadar, Bombay 400 028.
The annual subscription rate for 24 issues is Rs. 72/- per year (add Rs. 5/- on outstation cheques). Drafts/cheques/M.O. should be in favour of PARTHA BOOKS DIVISION.

Readers' Contributions should be addressed to Editor, TINKLE, Mahalaxmi Chambers (Basement), 22 Bhulabhai Desai Road, Bombay 400 026.

Mooshik:
Rs. 10/- will be paid for every original idea accepted.

Readers' Choice:
* Please send only folktales you have heard and not those you have read in books, magazines or textbooks. Rs. 25/- will be paid for every accepted contribution.
* Send a self-addressed stamped envelope if you want the story to be returned.
* Please do not send photographs until asked for.

This happened to me:
You can write on your own strange, thrilling or amusing experience or adventure. Rs. 15/- will be paid for every accepted contribution

Readers Write...
1. Mail your letters to: Tinkle, P. Bag No. 16541, Bombay 400 026.
2. Please give your address in your letters, if you want a reply.

TINKLE TRICKS AND TREATS
1. Mail your entry to: Tinkle Competition Section, P. Bag No. 16541, Bombay 400 026
2. The first 40 all-correct entries will each receive a **LEO** Scrambler costing Rs. 29/- from M/s. Blow Plast Ltd., P.O. Box No. 9145, Bombay 25.
3. The next 350 all-correct entries received by us will each win a copy of the AMAR INDIA WALL PAPER NO. 20.

*Refer to the footnote under the Editor's Note

- - - CUT HERE - - -

ENTRY FORM*   TTT-36

NAME _____

Answer: _____

ADDRESS _____

STATE _____

PIN _____

Nasruddin Hodja

Readers Write...*

If you don't mind, I wish to complain about TINKLE No. 38. "The Naughty Smile" was a very silly story. I hope you won't publish stories like this again, otherwise I will be very angry.

Melvin Krupakar
Hyderabad

In TINKLE No. 39 you have told us how to take care of cats. But I have a dog! So please publish a feature on how to take care of dogs.

Meena
Bombay

I am very fond of Nasruddin Hodja, but I'm disappointed at not finding him in recent issues of TINKLE. Has he taken a vacation or has he been retired? I hope the former so that he will reappear soon.

Manish Pandeya
Jamshedpur

Why don't you publish a super poster of Kalia, Doob-doob, Chamataka and Babloo?

Saponti Baroowa
Golaghat

I'm in the VIth standard and your feature on the Moon has helped me a lot in my General Science class.

Dinesh Parab
Bombay

I was astonished to see the feature on the Moon – Our Strange Neighbour, in TINKLE No. 38. I showed it to my parents and friends and they were excited to read it. In fact everyone was thrilled with the feature. So thank you very much.

A. Guru Prasad
Udupi

I wish I had a "magic pot" (TINKLE No.39) so that I could sit all day and produce thousands of TINKLE magazines and distribute them to all my friends!

Vijay Hattiholi
Dharwar

(I am so pleased with your reply that I have sent you ten back issues free. Give them away!
– Editor)

C The boy is puzzled by the markings on the crates. Can you tell him what the markings (the arrows, the umbrella and the broken glass) stand for?

D # MAKE A COLOURFUL DUSTBIN

You will need:
1. An old tin—cleaned thoroughly
2. Strips of colourful cloth or paper
3. Glue
4. Lace

Method:

a. Keep the tin upright on the paper or cloth and cut a round shape to fit the bottom.

b. Wrap the fabric round the tin to see how much you should cut.

c. Unwrap the fabric from the tin and cut the length you require.

d. Glue the fabric round the tin.

e. Glue the round shape you have cut out from the fabric to the bottom of the tin.

f. Cut out pictures of flowers from old greeting cards and stick them on the tin.

g. Glue lace neatly all around the rim.

Your dustbin is now ready for use!

THE MONKEY'S DANCE
Illustrations: V.B. Halbe

READERS' CHOICE

Based on a story sent by Asharam Apoom, Shillong

THE SUN
Script: J.D. Isloor
Illustrations: Anand Mande

YOU CAN SEE SEVERAL STARS IN THE SKY AT NIGHT...

...BUT IN THE DAYTIME, THE ONLY STAR YOU CAN SEE IS THE SUN.

IF THE SUN IS A STAR WHY DOESN'T IT LOOK LIKE OTHER STARS? WHY DOES IT LOOK LIKE A HUGE RED BALL? THE SUN LOOKS DIFFERENT FROM OTHER STARS BECAUSE IT IS MILLIONS OF TIMES CLOSER TO EARTH THAN ANY OTHER STAR. IF OUR SUN WERE AS FAR AWAY AS THE OTHER STARS, IT TOO, WOULD HAVE APPEARED TO US AS A TWINKLING SPECK IN THE SKY.

AFTER THE SUN THE NEXT CLOSEST STAR IS PROXIMA CENTAURI.

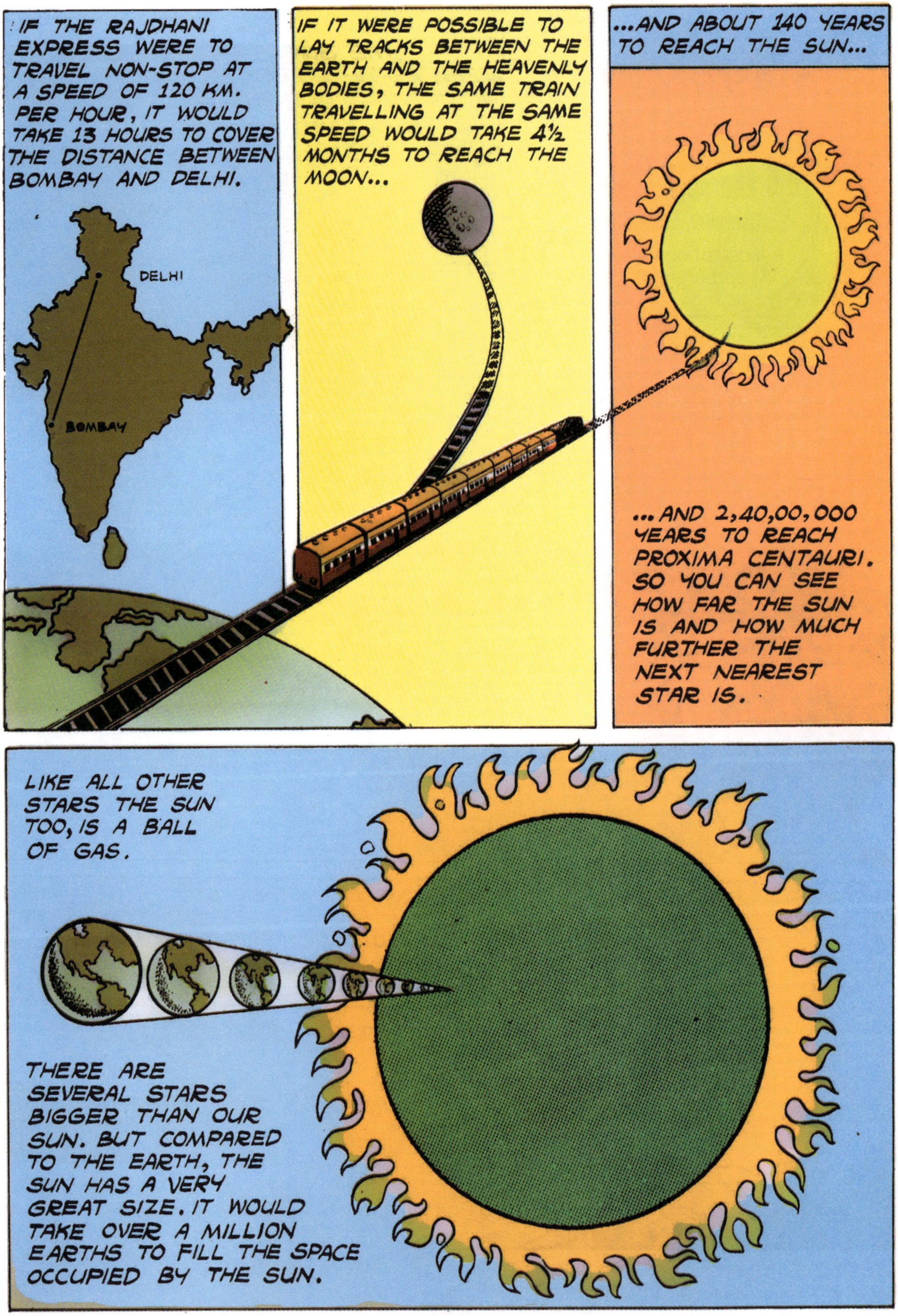

IF THE RAJDHANI EXPRESS WERE TO TRAVEL NON-STOP AT A SPEED OF 120 KM. PER HOUR, IT WOULD TAKE 13 HOURS TO COVER THE DISTANCE BETWEEN BOMBAY AND DELHI.

IF IT WERE POSSIBLE TO LAY TRACKS BETWEEN THE EARTH AND THE HEAVENLY BODIES, THE SAME TRAIN TRAVELLING AT THE SAME SPEED WOULD TAKE 4½ MONTHS TO REACH THE MOON...

...AND ABOUT 140 YEARS TO REACH THE SUN...

...AND 2,40,00,000 YEARS TO REACH PROXIMA CENTAURI. SO YOU CAN SEE HOW FAR THE SUN IS AND HOW MUCH FURTHER THE NEXT NEAREST STAR IS.

LIKE ALL OTHER STARS THE SUN TOO, IS A BALL OF GAS.

THERE ARE SEVERAL STARS BIGGER THAN OUR SUN. BUT COMPARED TO THE EARTH, THE SUN HAS A VERY GREAT SIZE. IT WOULD TAKE OVER A MILLION EARTHS TO FILL THE SPACE OCCUPIED BY THE SUN.

HOW THE TITEERI TOOK TO WATER
Illustrations: M. Mohandas

READERS' CHOICE
Based on a story sent by Aditya Vij, New Delhi

Raghu
Based on an idea suggested by V. Venkatesh, Bangalore

Results of Say it Yourself* No. 3

First Prize (Rs 50)
J. Meera
C/o. P. N. Jagannathan
5, Ayyavu Street
Shenoy Nagar
Madras 600 030

Second Prize (Rs. 25)
Khan Mohammad Tariq
"Marydale" Flat No. 6
2nd Floor, 25th Road
T.P.S. III, Bandra
Bombay 400 050

Third Prize (Rs. 15)
Ninad A. Kamat
D-10 Gayatri Apartments
Mahadevbhai Apartments
Mahadevbhai Desai Road
Borivli East
Bombay 400 066

CONSOLATION PRIZES OF RS: 10 EACH

Nassim Missaghtan — Goa
Mohit Mital — Baroda
Gautam Bothra — Calcutta
Sandeep B. Satam — Bombay
Amit K. Kothari — Bombay
Sriram Vishwanath — Surat
T. E. Shreedevi — Bombay
Mamta L. Sampat — Raichur
Apati Mohanram — Calcutta
N. Jackson Jacob — Ulhasnagar

Prize-winning entry from J. Meera

* Refer to the footnote under the Editor's Note

Mooshik
Based on an idea suggested by Rajesh Shetty, Bombay

IN THE FORESTS OF AFRICA A LONE HORNBILL OFTEN FOLLOWS A FAMILY OF CHATTERING GUENON MONKEYS. THE MONKEYS MOVE THROUGH THE HIGH TREES FEEDING ON FRUIT. IN THE PROCESS THEY STIR UP BEETLES, MOTHS AND OTHER INSECTS WHICH ARE SNAPPED UP BY THE HORNBILL. SOME SAY THE BIRD WARNS THE MONKEYS WHEN THERE IS DANGER AROUND.

THE SOOTY SHEARWATER MAKES ITS NEST IN A BURROW. SOON A TUATARA MAY COME TO LIVE WITH IT. THE SHEARWATER DOESN'T MIND. THE BIRD IS OUT HUNTING THE WHOLE DAY AND THE SLOW-MOVING REPTILE IS OUT HUNTING THE WHOLE NIGHT. SO THE TWO DON'T GET IN EACH OTHER'S WAY.

IN RETURN FOR THE BIRD'S HOSPITALITY, THE REPTILE CLEANS THE NEST OF BEETLES, CENTIPEDES AND FLIES.

IF THERE ARE NESTLINGS, HOWEVER, THE TUATARA MAY SOMETIMES GIVE IN TO TEMPTATION AND EAT ONE OF THE BABIES.

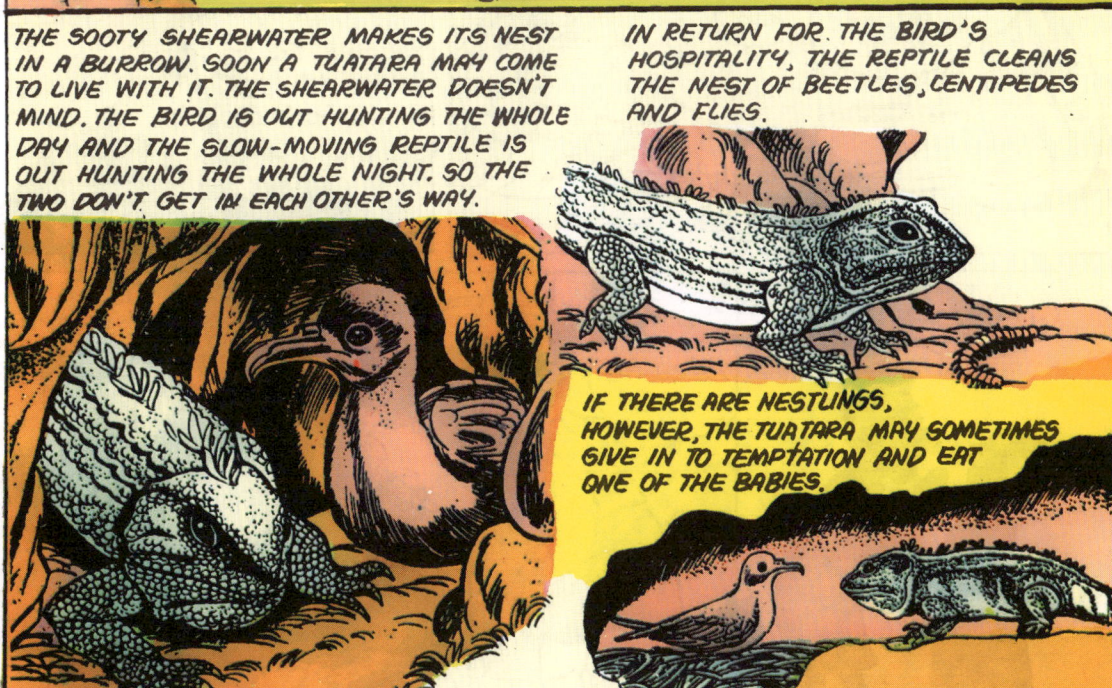

THE TRICK THAT FAILED

READERS' CHOICE

Based on a story sent by Ken, Kohima

Illustrations: V.B. Halbe

THE WISE KING

READERS' CHOICE

Illustrations: H.S. Chavan

Based on a story sent by Sumon Bhattacharjee, Shillong

LONG AGO, THE STATES NOW CALLED BENGAL, BIHAR AND ORISSA, WERE RULED BY KING RAMANA.

HE WAS A VERY ABLE KING AND WAS DEEPLY LOVED AND RESPECTED BY HIS SUBJECTS.

ONE DAY—

MAHARAJ, I BRING BAD NEWS.

YOUR ENEMIES IN ORISSA HAVE RISEN IN REVOLT AGAINST YOU.

I WILL MARCH AGAINST THOSE WHO HAVE REVOLTED.

MY PEOPLE, I GIVE YOU MY WORD THAT I WILL DESTROY THESE ENEMIES OF OUR LAND!

KING RAMANA'S ARMY MARCHED AGAINST THE REBELS AND EMERGED VICTORIOUS.

ABOUT
SAY IT YOURSELF

Kids say the craziest things. Just like the beloved *Tinkle* Toon Anwar, kids have a way of coming up with the most unexpected and cheeky replies to ordinary questions. But their cheeky wit is often lost when it comes to putting their thoughts in words. In July of 1983 *Tinkle* started a contest to encourage that very cheekiness.

The *Tinkle* editors believed that kids should not be constantly corrected while expressing themselves. This could curb their creativity and make them conform to what is expected of them. The question was, when creativity is encouraged in music and dance, why not treat writing the same way?

Tinkle's Associate Editor Mr. Subba Rao observed that when most kids write, they are so focused on being correct and being able to articulate that their emotions are left out of their words. He believed that kids need some help in transferring their ability to jibber-jabber to paper. This was the idea behind Say It Yourself.

Kids were given a three-panel gag with one speech bubble at the end left empty. They were expected to fill in the bubble with the wittiest answer or repartee they could think of. The best entries were given a prize. Kids embraced the opportunity and letters with funny and clever answers started arriving from across the country.

Say It Yourself remains, to this day, one of the most popular *Tinkle* features. This just goes to prove that, when given the chance, kids have a lot to say.

Mooshik
Based on an idea suggested by Jyoti Cardoza, Bombay

Readers Write...

I am a regular reader of TINKLE and have made a name for myself as a "good story-teller"! I read good stories in TINKLE and retell them to the great appreciation of my listeners.

N. Gokul Muthu
Virudhunagar

I like reading TINKLE, but after two weeks the front cover gets torn. Please use better quality cover paper.

C. K. Shahina
Malappuram

The Moon – Our Strange Neighbour in TINKLE is very informative. I hope you will publish a lot more on science.

Shakeer Ahmed
Bhatkal

One day I took two issues of TINKLE to class. Our teacher confiscated them. But after she had read them herself, she was happy. She returned them to me saying, "I am giving these books back to you because they are not really comics, but meaningful books!"

Marianne Menezes
Pune

In TINKLE No. 41 you wrote about speed. You mentioned that man has not yet built a machine to equal the speed of lightning. What about "thinking"? Isn't thinking faster than lightning?

P. Devairakkam
Bombay

(Tulsidas, a great poet of India, while describing the speed of Hanuman, says, "Hanuman went faster than a deer; faster than wind; nay, faster than mind itself."

– Editor)

Raghu
Based on an idea sent by V. Venkatesh, Bangalore

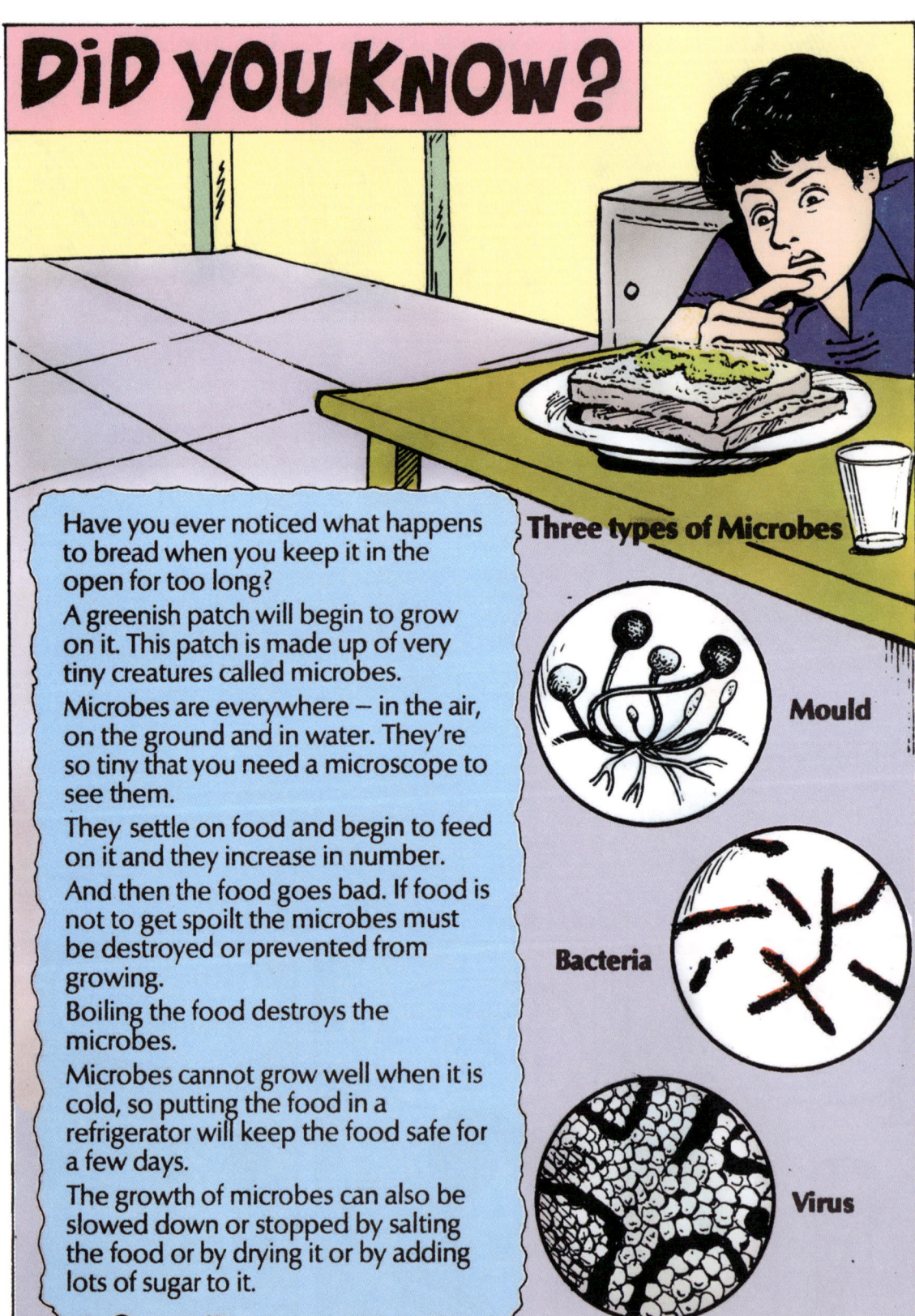

DID YOU KNOW?

Three types of Microbes

- Mould
- Bacteria
- Virus

Have you ever noticed what happens to bread when you keep it in the open for too long?

A greenish patch will begin to grow on it. This patch is made up of very tiny creatures called microbes.

Microbes are everywhere – in the air, on the ground and in water. They're so tiny that you need a microscope to see them.

They settle on food and begin to feed on it and they increase in number.

And then the food goes bad. If food is not to get spoilt the microbes must be destroyed or prevented from growing.

Boiling the food destroys the microbes.

Microbes cannot grow well when it is cold, so putting the food in a refrigerator will keep the food safe for a few days.

The growth of microbes can also be slowed down or stopped by salting the food or by drying it or by adding lots of sugar to it.

SAY IT YOURSELF AND WIN A CASH PRIZE* NO. 5

WHAT IS THE BOY'S ANSWER?

1. Mail your entry to:
   TINKLE
   Competition Section,
   P. Bag No. 16541
   Bombay 400 026

2. • First prize — Rs. 50/-
   • Second prize — Rs. 25/-
   • Third prize — Rs. 15/-
   • 10 Consolation prizes, — Rs. 10/- each

3. Decision of the judges is final and binding. Names of the prize-winners will be announced in TINKLE No. 51.

Last date for receiving entries: December 10, 1983

* Refer to the footnote under the Editor's Note

- CUT HERE

ENTRY FORM*   Say it Yourself – 5

NAME _____

Answer: _____

ADDRESS _____

STATE _____

PIN _____

PAKODAS FOR THE BEAR

Illustrations: Ashok Dongre

Readers' Choice

Based on a story sent by F.I. Farooqui, Bombay

EGGS

Script and Illustrations: Pradeep Sathe

A FERTILISED EGG IS ONE LAID BY A HEN AFTER MATING WITH A ROOSTER. A HEN CAN LAY AN EGG WITHOUT MATING WITH A ROOSTER TOO. THIS IS AN UNFERTILISED EGG. SOME PEOPLE CALL SUCH AN EGG A VEGETARIAN EGG. THIS EGG CANNOT HATCH INTO A CHICKEN, BUT IT HAS THE SAME FOOD VALUE (PROTEINS) AS A FERTILISED EGG.

UNFERTILISED EGG

FERTILISED EGG

THIS IS A FRESHLY-LAID FERTILISED EGG. THE CHICKEN HAS ALREADY STARTED FORMING INSIDE IT. IT IS A TINY SPECK, BUT LIKE ALL LIVING THINGS, IT NEEDS AIR.
AIR ENTERS EGGS THROUGH TINY PORES IN THEIR SHELLS. — PORES

ALBUMEN (WHITE) — YOLK — SHELL — BEGINNING OF CHICK — AIR POCKET

IF THE EGG IS KEPT WARM EITHER BY THE BIRD (HEN) OR IN AN INCUBATOR*...
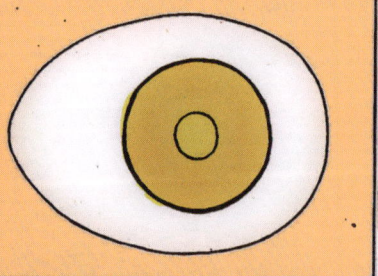

...THE TINY SPECK OF LIFE INSIDE IT STARTS FORMING INTO A CHICK.
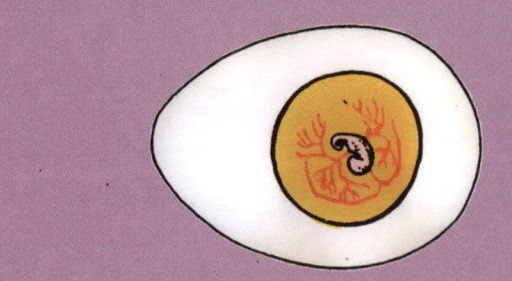

THIS IS HOW THE CHICK INSIDE LOOKS ON THE 5TH DAY.
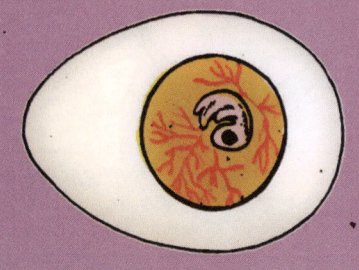

FOOD FROM THE YOLK IS FED TO THE CHICK THROUGH THIN BLOOD VESSELS.
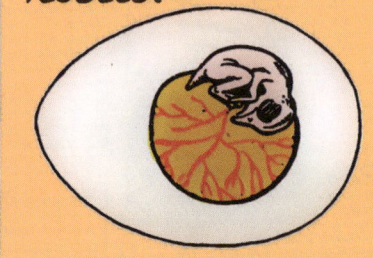

*INCUBATOR: A MACHINE TO HATCH EGGS.

BY THE 15TH DAY, THE YOLK IS REDUCED. THE CHICK'S EYES, BEAK AND FEET ARE DEVELOPED.

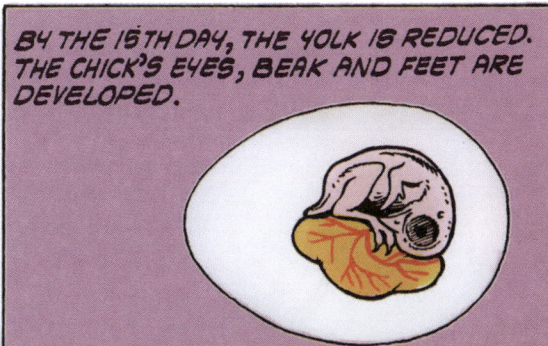

BY THE 20TH DAY, THE LEGS OF THE CHICK ARE STRONG ENOUGH TO STAND ON AND IT HAS DEVELOPED A TINY EGG-TOOTH ON THE BILL. ITS BODY GETS COVERED BY FINE SOFT FEATHERS.

ON THE 21ST DAY, WITH THE HELP OF THE EGG-TOOTH THE CHICK CRACKS THE EGG-SHELL AND COMES OUT. BUT IT IS WET AND STILL NEEDS SOME HEAT.

WITHIN AN HOUR ITS DOWN BECOMES DRY; ITS EGG-TOOTH TOO, FALLS OFF. AND A CUTE LITTLE CHICK LOOKS CURIOUSLY AT THE NEW WORLD.

LIKE HENS, OTHER BIRDS, TOO, LAY EGGS. DIFFERENT BIRDS LAY EGGS OF DIFFERENT SIZES. THE HUMMING BIRD LAYS A TINY EGG. THE LARGEST EGG IS LAID BY THE OSTRICH. THE OSTRICH'S EGG WEIGHS OVER 1 KG.
THE HATCHING PERIOD, TOO, IS DIFFERENT FOR DIFFERENT BIRDS.

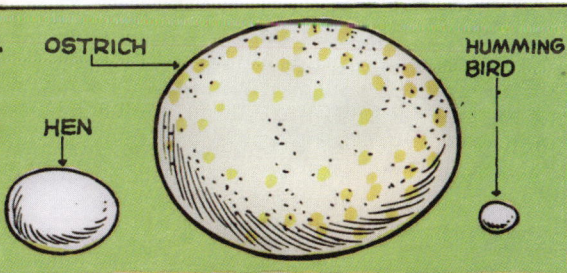

THE BUSH TURKEY OF AUSTRALIA PRODUCES THE MOST WELL-DEVELOPED CHICK. THE CHICK DEVELOPS WINGS AND FEATHERS WHILE STILL IN THE EGG.

ON THE OTHER HAND, THE CHICKS OF SOME BIRDS (SPARROWS, CROWS, KOELS ETC.) ARE HELPLESS WHEN THEY EMERGE FROM THE EGGS. THEY ARE NAKED (WITHOUT DOWN) AND BLIND. AND THEY ARE UNABLE TO WALK.

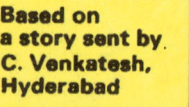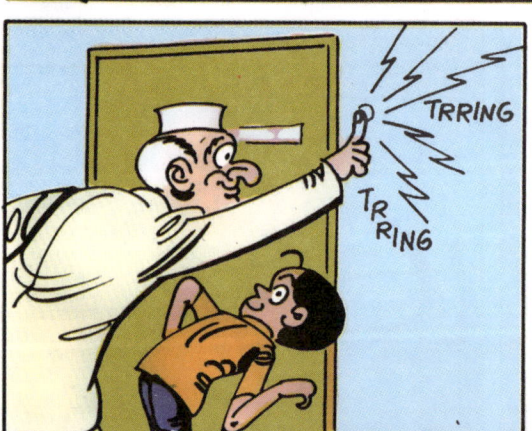

* Refer to the footnote under the Editor's Note

Chetak

Script: Luis M. Fernandes
Illustrations: Pradeep Sathe

IN 1576 A GREAT BATTLE WAS FOUGHT AT HALDIGHATI BETWEEN THE RAJPUTS AND THE MUGHALS.

THE RAJPUTS WERE LED BY RANA PRATAP...

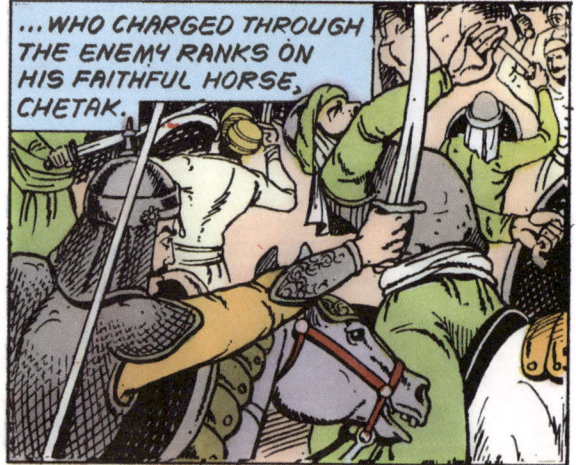

...WHO CHARGED THROUGH THE ENEMY RANKS ON HIS FAITHFUL HORSE, CHETAK.

MASTER AND HORSE FOUGHT AS A TEAM.

AEEII!

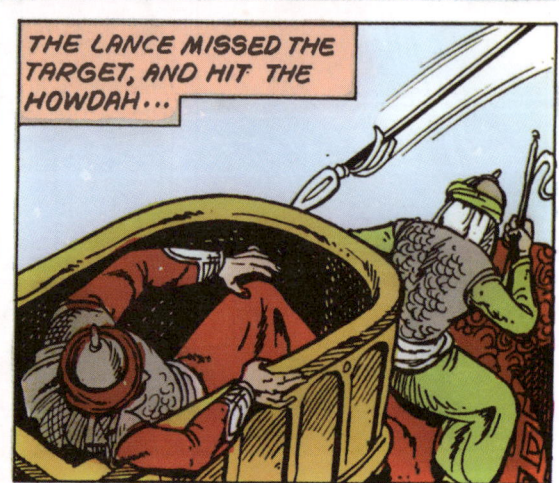

WIT OF VIJAYARAJ

READERS' CHOICE
Illustrations: M. Mohandas
Based on a story sent by Santosh and Dhiraj Sharma, Coimbatore

ONCE UPON A TIME, IN SOUTHERN INDIA, THERE WAS A KING CALLED VIJAYARAJ. ONE DAY HIS KINGDOM WAS ATTACKED BY THE SULTAN OF A NEIGHBOURING COUNTRY.

VIJAYARAJ AND HIS MEN FOUGHT BRAVELY BUT FINALLY LOST TO THE SULTAN.

"I ADMIRE YOU FOR YOUR BRAVERY, BUT YOU WILL HAVE TO DIE. DO YOU HAVE A LAST WISH?"

"YES, I WISH TO DRINK A CUP OF WATER."

"IS THAT ALL? SOLDIER, BRING WATER!"

"султAN, PLEASE ORDER YOUR MEN NOT TO KILL ME UNTIL I HAVE FINISHED THIS WATER."

"NO ONE WILL TOUCH YOU TILL YOU FINISH DRINKING."

VIJAYARAJ IMMEDIATELY POURED OUT THE WATER ON THE SANDY FLOOR.

"YOU MUST LET ME LIVE, NOW THAT I CAN'T DRINK IT ANYMORE!"

THE SULTAN THOUGHT IT OVER AND THEN LAUGHED.

"YOU'RE AS CLEVER AS YOU'RE BRAVE! NOW DRINK THIS WATER AND LIVE."

THE SULTAN RETURNED VIJAYARAJ'S KINGDOM TO HIM. AND THE TWO MEN BECAME GOOD FRIENDS.

ODD Friends – 2

Script: Ashvin
Illustrations: M. Mohandas

IN THE NESTING SEASON WHEN THE RUFOUS WOODPECKER IS READY TO LAY ITS EGGS, IT CARVES OUT A HOME FOR ITSELF IN THE TOUGH FOOTBALL-SHAPED ANT NEST. THE ANTS NEVER ATTACK THE WOODPECKER AND DO NOT TOUCH THE EGGS, EVEN THOUGH THEY EAT OTHER BIRDS' EGGS. AND THE WOODPECKER IN TURN, DOESN'T EAT ANY OF THE ANTS.

THE HONEY-GUIDE BIRD OF CENTRAL AFRICA EATS BEESWAX. AND THE RATEL LOVES HONEY. THE BIRD LEADS THE RATEL TO THE HIVE BY CHIRPING AGAIN AND AGAIN AS IT FLIES AHEAD. THE RATEL RIPS OPEN THE HIVE AND NOSES OUT THE HONEY. AFTER THE RATEL HAS FINISHED, THE BIRD SETTLES DOWN TO EAT THE BEESWAX FROM THE HONEYCOMBS LEFT AROUND.

EDITOR'S CHOICE

My young friends,

A poem titled 'Love for a Friend' has been sent to me by Anitha Rajashekaran of Madras. Here it is for your reading pleasure:

My dog in the kitchen
  said, "Wuff, wuff, wuff!"
I gave him some biscuits,
  But he went away in a huff!

I thought he wanted milk
  And poured it in his cup.
But he didn't sniff it either,
  For he was a naughty little pup.

I went to the butcher's
  And bought him a bone.
He did not glance at it,
  But answered me in a bad tone.

I sank in a chair
  And wondered in despair.
For I love him so much
  And I've taken so much care.

A thought struck me—
  I had not allowed him to go
And play with his friend,
  The dog next door.

I took him out and let him play.
  He bounded and leapt with joy.
For nothing is better than a pal,
  Neither a bone, nor a toy.

      Affectionately yours,
      Uncle Pai

Anitha

SAY HELLO TO SULABHA THAKUR

Writers and illustrators alone did not help *Amar Chitra Katha* (ACK) and *Tinkle* build their legacy. Colouring and lettering artists also deserve a fair share of the credit. Ms. Sulabha Thakur was one of those colourists who brought stories to life with the deft strokes of her brush.

Ms. Thakur had obtained a diploma in commercial art from the J.J. School of Arts, Mumbai, and was working in advertising before her association with ACK began. One day in 1975, through a friend, she met Mr. Bhavani Shankar Goray, who was a freelance colourist for ACK. He introduced her to Mr. Anant Pai, founder-editor of ACK. Soon after, she began working for him as a freelancer. Her work can be seen in the titles *Sati and Shiva* and *Mahabharat*, among many others. In 1980 when Mr. Pai began *Tinkle*, she worked for the new magazine too. In the first 60-odd issues of *Tinkle*, she coloured several stories and illustrated a couple as well.

Before computers became commonplace, the work of a colourist was a tedious process. "After an artist illustrated a story on paper, it went to a photo studio to be photographed. The photograph was then reprinted on bromide paper*." Colouring on bromide paper was no easy feat. "If the bromide paper hadn't been washed properly during processing, any colours I applied would either not stick or change entirely." Later, bromides

were phased out in favour of photocopies. While colouring on them was easier, there were still some challenges. "Printers in those days could only print 26 colours. So I could use only those colours. I was limited in what I could do," she says.

Despite the difficulties, Ms. Thakur affirms she enjoyed working for *ACK* and *Tinkle*. She particularly liked colouring the various animal features and ace artist Ram Waeerkar's illustrations in *Tinkle*.

Even though Ms. Thakur is now retired, we still have her warm tones and hues to remind us of her invaluable contribution in making our childhood more colourful.

*Paper containing silver bromide which made it sensitive to light and suitable for enlargements

Mooshik
Based on an idea suggested by Ashish Poddar, Bombay

To Our Readers*

TINKLE SUBSCRIPTIONS :
All new subscriptions and renewals of the old ones are accepted at :

PARTHA BOOKS DIVISION
Nav Prabhat Chambers, Ranade Road, Dadar, Bombay 400 028.
The annual subscription rate for 24 issues is Rs. 72/- per year (add Rs. 5/- on outstation cheques). Drafts/cheques/M.O. should be in favour of PARTHA BOOKS DIVISION.

Readers' Contributions should be addressed to Editor, TINKLE, Mahalaxmi Chambers (Basement), 22 Bhulabhai Desai Road, Bombay 400 026.

Mooshik :
Rs. 10/- will be paid for every original idea accepted.

ATTENTION!
TINKLE-READERS OF BOMBAY

On December 11, at 10.00 A.M., there will be a quiz contest on Indian history and mythology (based on Amar Chitra Katha) at Hiniduja Auditrium, Charni Road. There will be also an entertainment programme on the occasion.

Hurry up! Collect your entry passes from TINKLE office at Mahalaxmi Chambers (Basement)

— Uncle Pai

TINKLE TRICKS AND TREATS

1. The first 40 all-correct entries received by us will each win a Leo Scrambler.

2. The next 350 all-correct entries received by us will each win a copy of the AMAR INDIA WALL PAPER No. 21

3. Mail your entry to:
Tinkle Competition Section
P. Bag No. 16541
Bombay 400 026

* Refer to the fcotnote under the Editor's Note

---- CUT HERE

ENTRY FORM*   TTT-37

NAME _____

ADDRESS _____

STATE _____

PIN _____

Answer: _____

Raghu
Based on an idea suggested by V. Venkatesh, Bangalore

Readers Write...

I am a regular reader of TINKLE and enjoy reading it very much. My mother's most important shopping item is TINKLE! Stories in TINKLE create a cheerful mood in the readers. I was the one who introduced TINKLE to my classmates and they now get it regularly.

P. Kala
Tiruchirapalli

I like TINKLE very much and my mother likes "Mooshik" very much. Whenever I bring TINKLE home my mother asks me to read out "Mooshik" to her. She really enjoys it.

Karan P. Jotwani
Bombay

Going Down Poverty Lane

Once, when going for a walk,
I saw a little boy—
Staring at a rich man's child,
Who was busy with a toy.

Toys were not what the boy wanted,
His needs were very small.
He only asked for crumbs of bread,
For this; to each man, he would call.

No one heard his cries,
But instead fed their dogs.
The poor boy stared on,
His tears dissolving in the fog.

He then started crying,
And asked God of his sin.
Clutching his precious possessions,
A tattered shirt and a battered tin.

Sonia Manchanda
New Delhi

Mooshik
From an idea suggested by Lavino Pinheiro, Goa

TINKLE TRICKS & TREATS*
TTT-37

A What game are they playing?

B How many triangles are there in this picture?

C What is the name of this insect? And how does it travel?

* Refer to the footnote under the Editor's Note

SOLUTIONS TO TTT-37

A—Water Polo B—Thirteen C—Praying Mantis. It flies.

ORIGAMI-Hen — Mrs. Indu Tilak and Mrs. Gita Kantawala

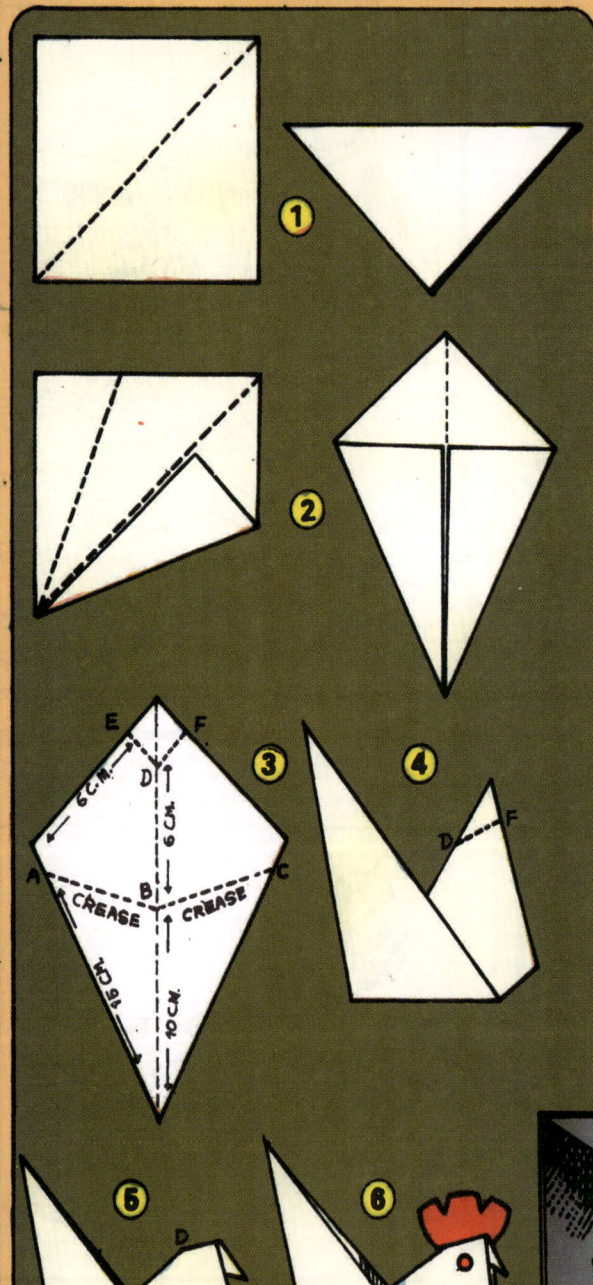

1. Take a 15 cm. square of yellow ochre paper and fold it into half.

2. Open out the paper and fold in the two side flaps as shown.

3. Turn it over and make deep creases, (AB) and (BC); and (DE) and (DF).

4. Fold up at (AB) and (BC).

5. Fold in the paper at DE and DF to make the beak.

6. Make cut-outs for eyes and comb of hen and stick them on.

Make 3-4 hens of different sizes so that you have a family. Take an old box, put some dry grass and ping-pong balls (to represent eggs) in, and you'll have a toy barn to show your friends.

THE SUN-II

Script: J.D. Isloor
Illustrations: Anand Mande

IT IS VERY HOT IN MAY.

THE TEMPERATURE AT THIS TIME IS BETWEEN 35°C TO 40°C.

YOU CAN IMAGINE HOW HOT IT MUST BE WHEN THE TEMERATURE IS 6000°C. THAT IS THE TEMPERATURE AT THE OUTSIDE OF THE SUN. THE OUTSIDE IS KEPT HOT BY HEAT COMING FROM DEEP INSIDE THE SUN. THE TEMPERATURE AT THE CENTRE OF THE SUN IS 14,000,000°C.

YOU MAY NOT BELIEVE IT, BUT THAT RAY OF LIGHT COMING IN THROUGH YOUR WINDOW WAS FORMED IN THE CENTRE OF THE SUN THOUSANDS OF YEARS AGO.

IT TOOK SO LONG TO REACH THE EARTH BECAUSE IT HAD A HARD TIME COMING TO THE SURFACE OF THE SUN. IT KEPT BUMPING INTO GAS PARTICLES AND HAD TO ZIG-ZAG INSIDE THE SUN FOR CENTURIES AND CENTURIES. FINALLY IT MANAGED TO ESCAPE TO THE SURFACE AND RACED TO THE EARTH. IT TOOK ABOUT EIGHT MINUTES TO COVER THE DISTANCE BETWEEN THE SURFACE OF THE SUN AND YOUR WINDOW.

BESIDES LIGHT, THE SUN GIVES OFF SOME HARMFUL RAYS, TOO. FORTUNATELY FOR US, OUR ATMOSPHERE, WHICH IS LIKE A PROTECTIVE BLANKET COVERING THE EARTH, ABSORBS THESE DANGEROUS RAYS AND PREVENTS THEM FROM REACHING US.

THE SUN'S SURFACE IS CONTINUALLY IN MOTION AND TONGUES OF FLAME LEAP OUTWARDS. THESE TONGUES OF FLAME ARE CALLED PROMINENCES. THEY ARE REALLY VISIBLE ONLY DURING AN ECLIPSE. SOMETIMES THESE PROMINENCES REACH OUT THOUSANDS OF KILOMETRES INTO SPACE.

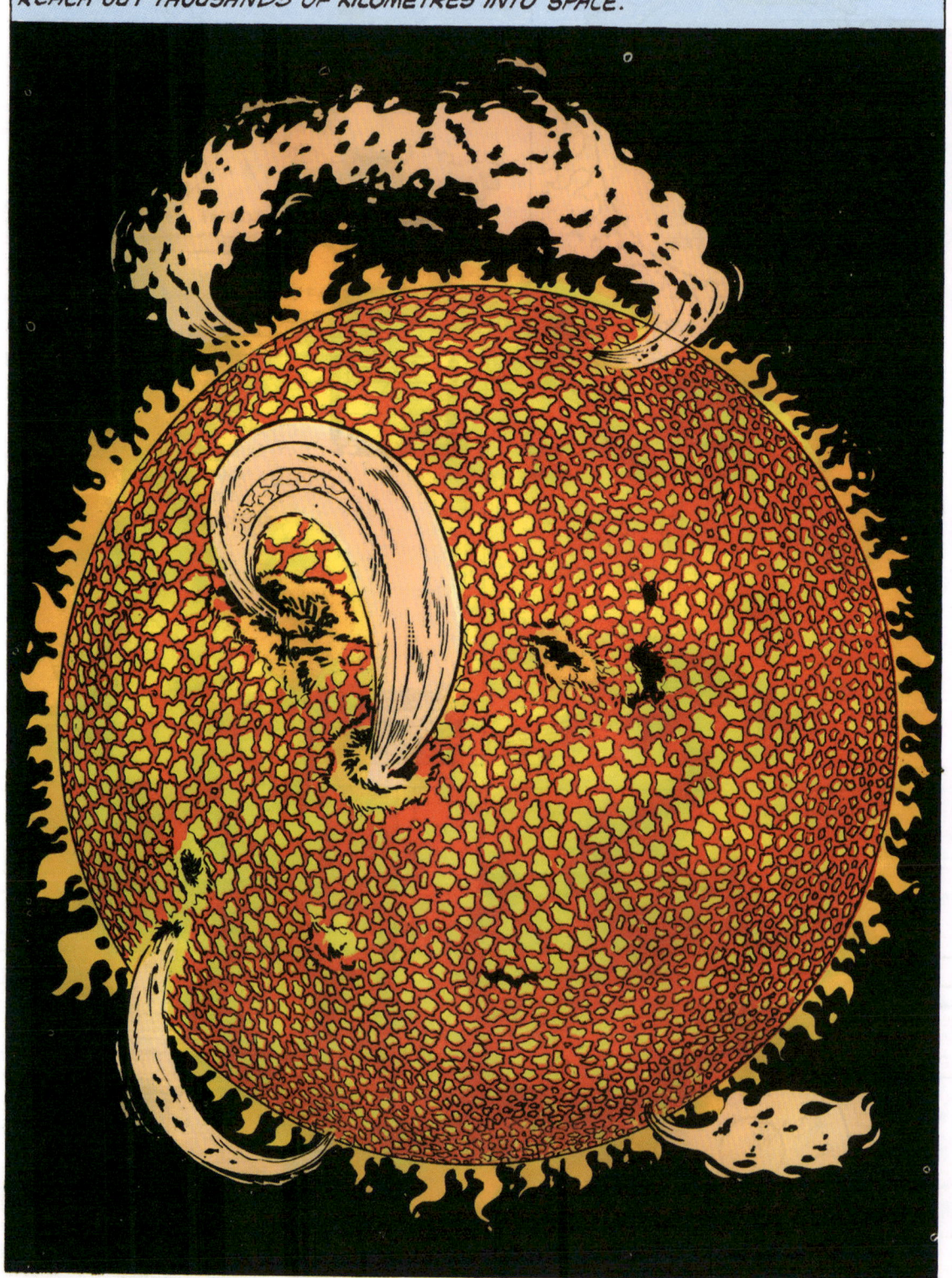

DISTURBANCES ON THE SUN CAN AFFECT THE EARTH TOO. ON 12TH NOVEMBER, 1960 THERE WAS A GREAT EXPLOSION ON THE SUN. SIX HOURS LATER A GIGANTIC CLOUD OF HYDROGEN GAS FLYING OUT FROM THE SUN, COLLIDED WITH THE EARTH AT A SPEED OF ABOUT 6400 KM. A SECOND.

FOR HOURS ALL LONG-DISTANCE RADIO COMMUNICATIONS WERE BLACKED OUT.

...COMPASS NEEDLES WENT HAYWIRE.

AEROPLANE PILOTS LOST CONTACT WITH THEIR GROUND STATIONS...

IN SOME PARTS OF THE WORLD ELECTRIC LIGHTS FLICKERED AS IF IN A STORM. YET THE AIR AND SKY WERE CLEAR AND SILENT. SOME OF THE DISTURBANCES LASTED FOR MORE THAN A WEEK!

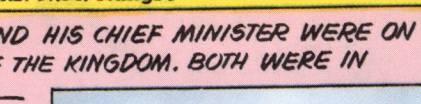

SILK COTTON TREE

Script: J.D. Isloor
Illustrations: Anand Mande

THE TREE GROWS VERY TALL WITH HORIZONTAL BRANCHES. THE LEAVES ARE EACH MADE UP OF 5-7 LEAFLETS.

THE SILK COTTON TREE IS ONE OF THE MOST GORGEOUS OF INDIAN TREES. IT IS ALSO KNOWN FOR ITS VERY LONG LIFE.

THE FLOWERS APPEAR IN JANUARY AND FEBRUARY. WHEN IN FULL BLOOM THE TREE PRESENTS A STRIKING BLAZE OF COLOUR. THE TREE BECOMES A PARADISE FOR BIRDS.

THE FRUITS APPEAR IN APRIL AND MAY. THE FRUITS SPLIT AND THE SOFT SILKY COTTON INSIDE IS BLOWN AWAY BY THE WIND.

THE WOOD IS SOFT AND LIGHT. IT IS USED FOR MAKING MATCH STICKS, TEA CHESTS, ETC.

THIS MAJESTIC TREE IS OFTEN MENTIONED IN SANSKRIT LITERATURE AS A RESTING PLACE FOR BIRDS AT NIGHT.

THE PINEAPPLE FRUIT BEARS AT ITS BASE AND TOP, A NUMBER OF YOUNG PLANTS. EACH ONE CAN BE SEPARATED AND GROWN INTO A NEW PLANT.

IN THE CASE OF PLANTS GROWING IN MARSHY AREAS OR NEAR SALT WATER, THE YOUNG PLANTS ARE BORN WITHIN THE FRUIT ITSELF. AFTER A CERTAIN PERIOD OF GROWTH, THE PLANT GETS SEPARATED FROM THE FRUIT AND DEVELOPS INTO A NEW PLANT.

YOUNG PLANTS GROWING OUT FROM FRUITS

RAMU AND THE RICKSHAW

Illustrations: Ram Waeerkar

READERS' CHOICE
Based on a story sent by Kumar Menon, Cochin

Mooshik

Based on an idea suggested by Juee, Bombay

Readers Write...

Could you start a feature on stamps and their origin? You could tell us about the stamps which have become rare and the first postage stamp which was issued in India and when.

Suhail Niaz
Calcutta

I am studying Sanskrit and my little knowledge tells me that the Sanskrit word for 'Mouse' is Mooshak and not Mooshik. Am I right?

Jyoti Chawla
New Delhi

(Yes, you are – Editor)

When my teacher asked me to write a composition on tigers, I wrote what I had read in TINKLE and I stood first! TINKLE is the most popular comic in our school.

K. Sanjay
Hyderabad

I love TINKLE. I suggest that you have a page full of jokes. I also suggest that you should have a TINKLE CLUB.

Sukoon Manekia
Bombay

I want Chamataka to eat at least two animals and laugh at Kalia.

Imran Khan
Mysore

There are several cases of child-lifting in the Pavgada district of Tumkur. I have a suggestion to make. Since most of these cases involve wolves, why don't you send our Dog Detective RANJHA to solve this baffling mystery? He would do so in less than a minute!

Upendra Babu
Bangalore

Thank you for publishing a feature on the dolphin in TINKLE No. 41. It proved helpful to me in school.

Asif Ali
Udupi

* Refer to the footnote under the Editor's Note

- - - CUT HERE - -

ENTRY FORM*

NAME _____

ADDRESS _____

STATE _____

PIN ☐☐☐☐☐☐

Say it Yourself – 6

Answer _____

DID YOU KNOW?

The game of chess originated in India.

Originally it was a game for four players and included the use of a dice to decide moves. It had a king-piece and four other types of pieces – an elephant, a horse, a chariot and four footmen – corresponding to the four corps of the ancient Indian army. It was called "chaturanga" or "four corps".

In the 6th century A.D. traders took the game to Persia where it became known as "shatranj". From Persia it moved to North Africa and Europe.

Akbar, it is said, played the game of "living chess" with maids acting as the chess pieces, moving on the open air chequered floor of the court at Fatehpur Sikri.

Today chess is a game of skill for only two players, played on a board divided into 64 alternating black and white squares, with 32 chessmen. It is played all over the world.

SAY IT YOURSELF AND WIN A CASH PRIZE* NO. 6

WHAT DOES THE BUS DRIVER SAY?

1. Mail your entry to:
   TINKLE Competition Section,
   P. Bag No. 16541 Bombay 400026
2. • First prize - Rs. 50/-   • Second prize - Rs. 25/-
   • Third prize - Rs. 15/-   • 10 Consolation prizes of Rs. 10/- each
3. Decision of the judges is final and binding. Names of the prize-winners will be announced in TINKLE No. 53
4. Entry form for Say It Yourself No. 6 is given on page No. 15

Last date for receiving entries: 10.1.1984

Results of Say It Yourself* No. 4

FIRST PRIZE (Rs. 50)	SECOND PRIZE (Rs. 25)	THIRD PRIZE (Rs. 15)
Debjani Dutta 47 Lansdowne Terrace Calcutta 700026	Poornima Audiseshu C/o. Wing Cdr. Audiseshu 196, Officer's Quarters A.F. Station Jamnagar 361003	Kunal Jha 133 Katari Baug Naval Base Cochin 682004

Consolation Prizes of Rs. 10 each

R. Dhyana Shobha Bangalore	Nanditha Nagaraj Madras	Purushottam Hyderabad
D. Mohan Krishna Secunderabad	D. Umashankar Bangalore	K. Ram Kumar Secunderabad
Ipshita Sen Gupta Cuttack	Ashutosh V. Bapat Bangalore	Shalini Gopal Visakhapatnam
		Karun Kumar Kak New Delhi

Prize-winning entry from Debjani Dutta

EDITOR'S CHOICE

My young friends,

The headman of Rangenhalli village had a son called Rangegowda. He was sent to the city to study. When he came back to the village for his holidays, his friends were eager to show the villagers how clever he was.

So one day they announced that Rangegowda would give a lecture and that everyone was welcome to come and listen.

A large crowd came to hear him speak. Rangegowda got up and asked the crowd whether they wanted to hear his speech in English or in Kannada. They all shouted back: "Eng-li-pice!"

Rangegowda cleared his throat and began: "ABC ... WXYZ ... ABC ... YZ ... ABCDEF ... XYZ ... ABCDE ... Z ... AB ...UVWXYZ!" all the time making wild gestures. Sometimes he spoke in harsh tones, sometimes softly. He continued for 15 minutes and then stopped.

There was loud and appreciative applause from the audience. Then one villager turned to another: "How well our young gowda speaks! But did you understand what he said?"

The other villager replied, "Where's the need to understand what he said when we SAW his speech!"

Affectionately yours,
Ananthihai
Uncle Pai

This story has been sent in by B.G. Sarvesh of Bangalore.

RAGHU

What if I told you that one of *Tinkle*'s wittiest toons is one of its youngest? Raghu had readers rolling on the floor with laughter. He was the quickest to the joke and always left adults scratching their head, so it's no wonder that everybody loved Raghu.

Raghu's rise to fame amongst *Tinkle* Toons is surprising when you consider his size. We aren't talking about Raghu's height here… no, we're referring to the size of his comic. Raghu had a three-panel comic. A three-panel comic that joined the likes of Mooshik and See & Smile in the magazine. It started as a page filler, a way to fill the empty space usually seen on reader feedback and contest pages. But Raghu soon rose in popularity. Raghu was quick-witted, which was something he needed to be, seeing as how he had only three panels to work with!

However, if you look back at all the old Raghu comics, you will find one unusual thread linking them all. Unlike most other *Tinkle* Toons, Raghu has been drawn by several different illustrators. Raghu was a stepping stone for artists once they joined *Tinkle*. Raghu offered illustrators the chance to try their hand at comics without going into the deep end of full-page and long stories. Archana Amberkar (currently illustrating Suppandi) got her start illustrating Raghu.

In fact, two of *Tinkle*'s most iconic illustrators, Ram Waeerkar and Vasant Halbe, also drew Raghu during their time with the magazine. Raghu became so popular that stories for him were sent in by readers from across the country, with many making it into the magazine. Everyone wanted to be Raghu and if they couldn't they at least wanted to write or draw him!

THE STETHOSCOPE

Script : Dr. N. N. Laha
Illustrations : Anand Mande

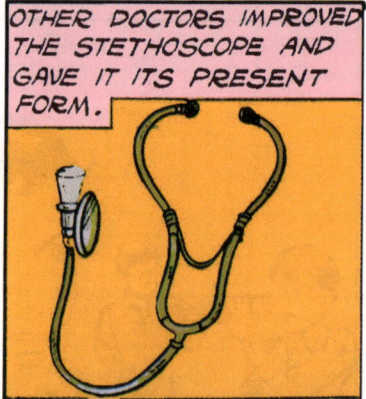

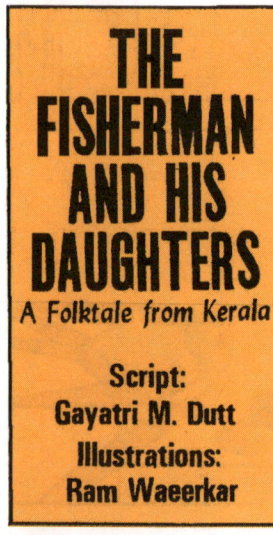

A CAT OR A DOG CAN DIG WITH ITS CLAWS. THE EARTHWORM DOESN'T HAVE CLAWS OR ANYTHING ELSE TO HELP IT DIG. SO IT JUST EATS ITS WAY THROUGH THE SOIL.

WHAT HAPPENS TO ALL THE SOIL IT SWALLOWS? IT THROWS IT OUT AS WASTE. THIS SOIL, HOWEVER, IS FERTILE AND IF THERE ARE THOUSANDS OF EARTHWORMS IN A FIELD AND IF ALL OF THEM BRING UP A LITTLE SOIL TO THE SURFACE, THE WHOLE FIELD BECOMES FERTILE IN COURSE OF TIME.

ALSO, THE BURROWS THAT THEY DIG ALLOW RAIN WATER TO GO DEEP DOWN INTO THE SOIL. AIR TOO, CAN GO INTO THE GROUND THROUGH THESE BURROWS. WHEN RAINWATER AND AIR CAN GO DOWN INTO THE EARTH, THE SOIL BECOMES RICHER AND PLANTS CAN GROW BETTER IN SUCH SOIL.

ANOTHER WAY IN WHICH EARTHWORMS IMPROVE THE SOIL IS BY ADDING MANURE TO IT. THIS THEY DO BY PULLING IN LEAVES WHICH ARE LYING NEAR THE ENTRANCE TO THEIR BURROWS. THEY EAT A PART OF THE LEAF AND USE THE REST TO LINE THE WALLS OF THE BURROW. THE LEAF ROTS AND PROVIDES NOURISHMENT TO THE SOIL.

THE HUMBLE EARTHWORM THEREFORE, IS A FRIEND OF MAN, HELPING HIM TO GROW CROPS BY ENRICHING THE SOIL.

EDITOR'S CHOICE

My young friends,

One winter a robin flew here and there looking for food. It soon felt tired and settled down on a cherry tree. The tree was bare of all fruit and leaves.

The robin suddenly noticed a snail crawling up the tree. "Why are you climbing this cherry tree, my friend?" asked the robin. "Don't you know there are no cherries at this time of year?"

"I know there are no cherries just now, but by the time I reach the top, there will be!" replied the snail.

"Ah! My friend, you are indeed very wise!" said the robin and flew off.

Affectionately yours,

Uncle Pai

This story has been sent in by Debashish Rao, Ganjam.

Mooshik
Based on an idea suggested by Jaideep Mehta, Bombay

To Our Readers*

TINKLE SUBSCRIPTIONS :
All new subscriptions and renewals of the old ones are accepted at :

PARTHA BOOKS DIVISION
Nav Prabhat Chambers, Ranade Road, Dadar, Bombay 400 028.
The annual subscription rate for 24 issues is Rs. 72/- per year (add Rs. 5/- on outstation cheques). Drafts/cheques/M.O. should be in favour of PARTHA BOOKS DIVISION.

Readers' Contributions should be addressed to Editor, TINKLE, Mahalaxmi Chambers (Basement), 22 Bhulabhai Desai Road, Bombay 400 026.

Mooshik :
Rs. 10/- will be paid for every original idea accepted.

Readers' Choice :
* Please send only folktales you have heard and not those you have read in books, magazines or textbooks. Rs. 25/- will be paid for every accepted contribution.
* Send a self-addressed stamped envelope if you want the story to be returned.
* Please do not send photographs until asked for.

This happened to me :
You can write on your own strange, thrilling or amusing experience or adventure. Rs. 15/- will be paid for every accepted contribution

Readers Write...
1. Mail your letters to: Tinkle, P. Bag No. 16541, Bombay 400 026.
2. Please give your address in your letters, if you want a reply.

TINKLE TRICKS AND TREATS

1. Mail your entry to : Tinkle Competition Section, P. Bag No. 16541, Bombay 400 026.
2. The first 50 all-correct entries received by us will each win a set of personal letterheads, with the winners' names and addresses printed on them !
3. The next 350 all-correct entries received by us will each win a copy of the AMAR INDIA WALL PAPER No. 22

* Refer to the footnote under the Editor's Note

CUT HERE

ENTRY FORM*   **TTT-38**

NAME _____

ADDRESS _____

STATE _____

PIN ___

Answer: _____

Readers Write...

I have no complaints about TINKLE! In issue No. 42 the story OH AND EH! was very good and so was Nasruddin Hodja.

Sudheendhra Putty
Secunderabad

Recently we had an essay writing competition on Ladybirds and I got first prize! All because of TINKLE!

R. V. Subramaniyan
Bangalore

I was sad to see that the feature on the Moon ended in TINKLE No. 42. Please continue to publish features on Space.

Suresh Chumbre
Belgaum

One day I brought a copy of TINKLE home. My father was very angry and told me to stick to my school books. But I told him to read it. He was so happy when he finished reading that he rushed out and came back with a whole bunch of TINKLE issues. Now he expects me to read TINKLE regularly to improve my general knowledge!

Ravi Valecha
Bombay

Our whole family has enjoyed DOG DETECTIVE RANJHA. But we want to know if the stories are true or not. Can you tell us?

Rakesh Parekh
Calicut

(The RANJHA stories are based on fact – Editor)

Could you please publish more Nasruddin Hodja stories? It's nice to read humorous stories in simple language.

Michael Siddhi
Kathmandu

I like TINKLE very much. Please place the entry form on the last page, separately. I don't like something to get torn from the middle of TINKLE.

Manoj Prithiani
Bombay

On the front cover of TINKLE No. 41 there is a picture of a monster. Sometimes very young readers may feel afraid on seeing such pictures!

A. J. Jophy
Bombay

Mooshik
Based on an idea suggested by Bonio D'cruz, Goa

TINKLE TRICKS & TREATS* TTT-38

A Put in the missing number.

B Two of these peacocks look exactly alike. Which two?

C This is an outline of the map of a country. Which one?

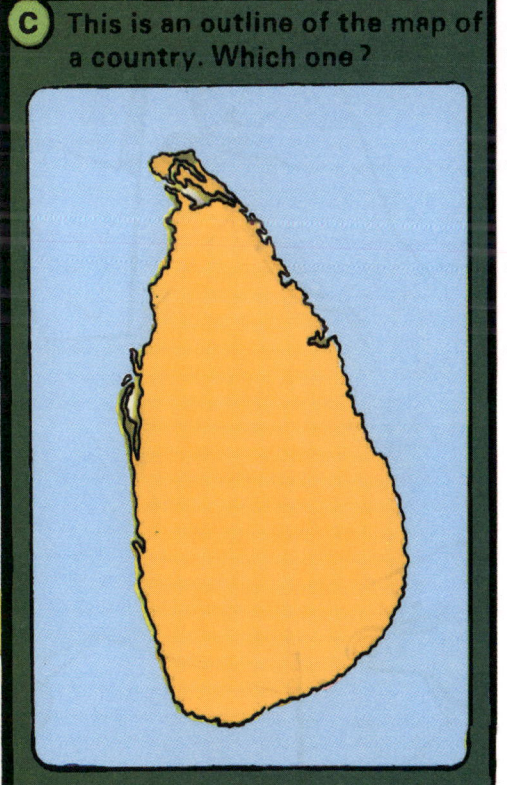

* Refer to the footnote under the Editor's Note

SOLUTIONS TO TTT-38
A. 10   B. 1 and 2   C. Sri Lanka

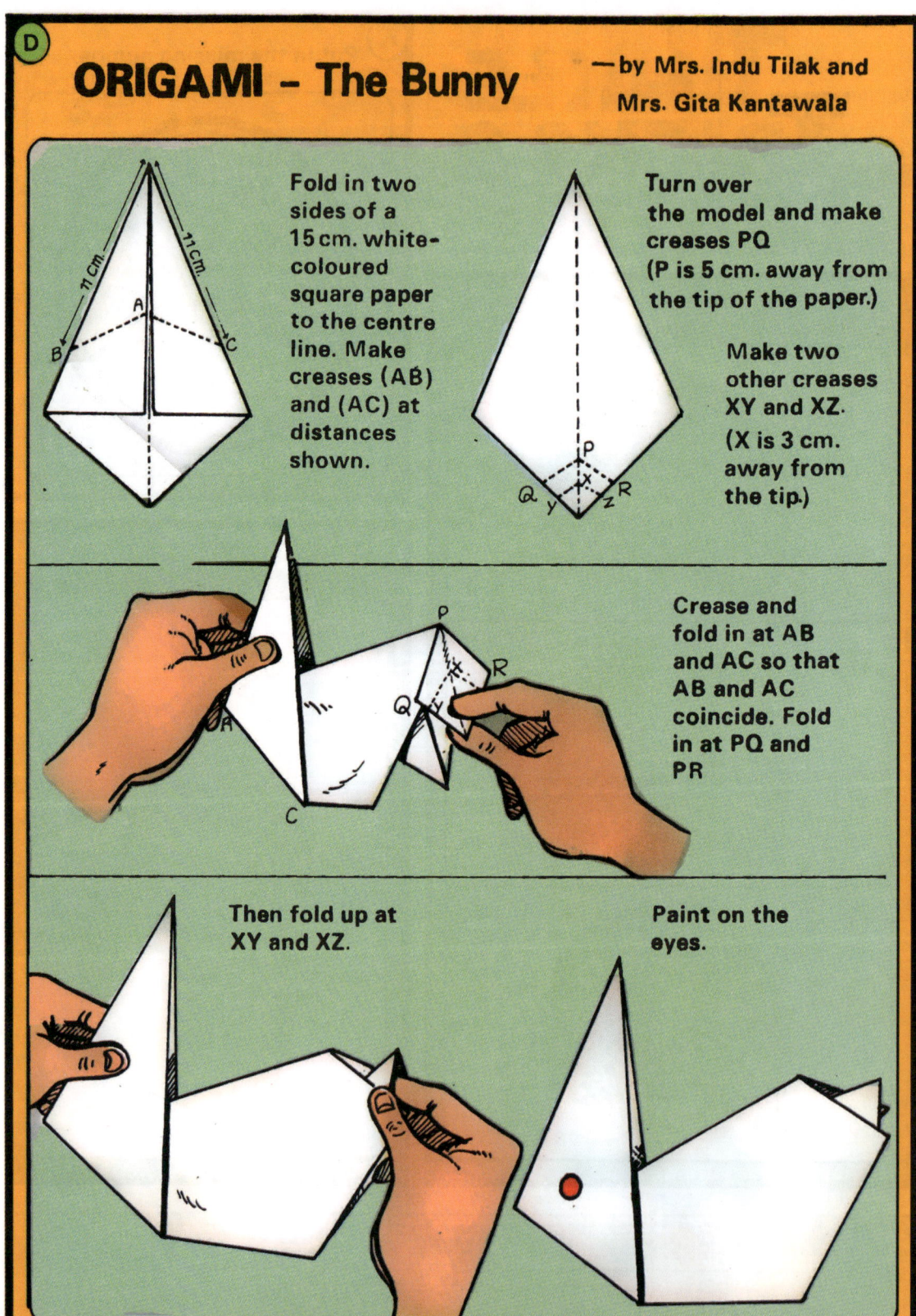

Worried you'll miss out on brand new Tinkle Stories?

Start a Subscription with us!

FRESH AND EXCITING STORIES

AMAZING D-I-Y PROJECTS

FASCINATING TRIVIA

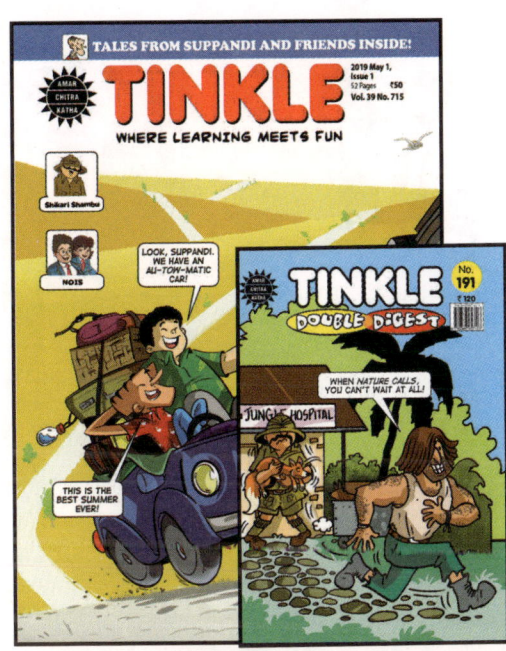

FUN FOR THE WHOLE FAMILY

UNINTERRUPTED TINKLE SUPPLY

DELIVERY BY COURIER

Product	Term	Issues	Cover Price	You Pay	Save	Complimentary Gifts
Tinkle Magazine	1 year	24	₹1200	₹999	₹301	Two Folk Tales comics free!
Tinkle Combo	1 year	24+12	₹2640	₹1999	₹741	Four Folk Tales comics free!

PLEASE ALLOW FOUR TO SIX WEEKS FOR YOUR SUBSCRIPTION TO BEGIN!

OFFER VALID TILL 31ST JULY, 2019

YOUR DETAILS

Full Name: .... Date of Birth: ☐☐ ☐☐ ☐☐☐☐

Address: ....

City: .... State: .... Pin Code: ☐☐☐☐☐☐

Phone/Mobile No.: ☐☐☐ ☐☐☐☐☐☐☐☐☐☐

Email: ....

Parent's Signature

PAYMENT OPTIONS

Cheque/DD: ☐☐☐☐☐☐ drawn in favour of 'ACK MEDIA DIRECT LTD.' on bank ....

.... for amount .... Dated: ☐☐ / ☐☐ / ☐☐

SEND US YOUR COMPLETED FORM WITH YOUR CHEQUE/DD AT:
ACK Media Direct Ltd, AFL House, 7th Floor, Lok Bharati Complex, Marol-Maroshi Road, Andheri (East), Mumbai 400 059.

MORE WAYS TO SUBSCRIBE: www.tinklesubs.com | customerservice@ack-media.com | +91-22-49188881/2

*T &C Apply